Doodle All Day
with Ladybug Girl

by David Soman
and Jacky Davis

P9-DBY-560

GROSSET & DUNLAP
Published by the Penguin Group
Penguin Group (USA) LLC, 375 Hudson Street, New York, New York 10014, USA

USA | Canada | UK | Ireland | Australia | New Zealand | India | South Africa | China

penguin.com
A Penguin Random House Company

ISBN 978-0-448-47859-3

10 9 8 7 6 5 4 3 2 1

Ladybug Girl loves flying her
kite at the beach!
Can you decorate it for her?

Ladybug Girl likes
trying on costumes,
but now her room is a mess!
What different costume pieces
does she have on her floor?

Ladybug Girl can do anything! She can swing across the monkey bars and hang upside down by her knees.

4

Draw Ladybug Girl's upside-down view of the park.

Ladybug Girl and Bingo love gardening!
Help them by drawing more plants and flowers in the garden.

Ladybug Girl and Bingo are having a tea party.
Can you draw some yummy treats for them to enjoy?

Ladybug Girl has invited you
to her birthday party.
Draw yourself joining the party!
Do you want to bring a present
or balloons?

Ladybug Girl and Bingo are building snow animals.
Can you help them make more?

Ladybug Girl and Bingo are off on an adventure to find a waterfall! Can you draw the waterfall and its rainbow spray?

The Bug Squad are preparing
for their next challenge.
But someone is missing!
Can you add Bumblebee Boy
to the squad?

Ladybug Girl has been busy building
a huge sand castle!
What does her sand castle look like?

The Bug Squad sees a silly alien in the house.
Can you draw what they see?

Bingo goes everywhere with Ladybug Girl!
But today he's run too far ahead of her.
Draw Bingo as he scratches, sniffs, runs, hides,
and jumps along the path.

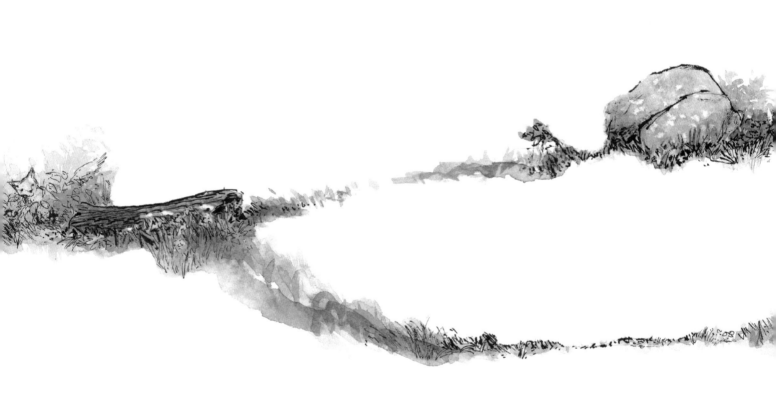

Mama and Ladybug Girl have taken Bingo out for a walk.
Can you draw any dogs they meet along the way?

Ladybug Girl and the Bug
Squad are on their way
to their special hideout
in the trees!
Draw what their secret
hideout looks like.

Ladybug Girl has made a whole picnic for her family!
Draw in the picnic blanket, the basket,
and the treats she has brought for them.

Bingo is hungry after running around with Ladybug Girl all morning! Can you feed Bingo a big bowl of kibble?

Watch out, robot—it's Bumblebee Boy! Draw the giant robot.

Lulu and her family have had a fun day at the beach,
but it's time to head home.

Can you draw the sunset and some boats on the water?

Ladybug Girl and Bingo are going to make
a big penguin by walking in the snow.
Can you help them finish it?

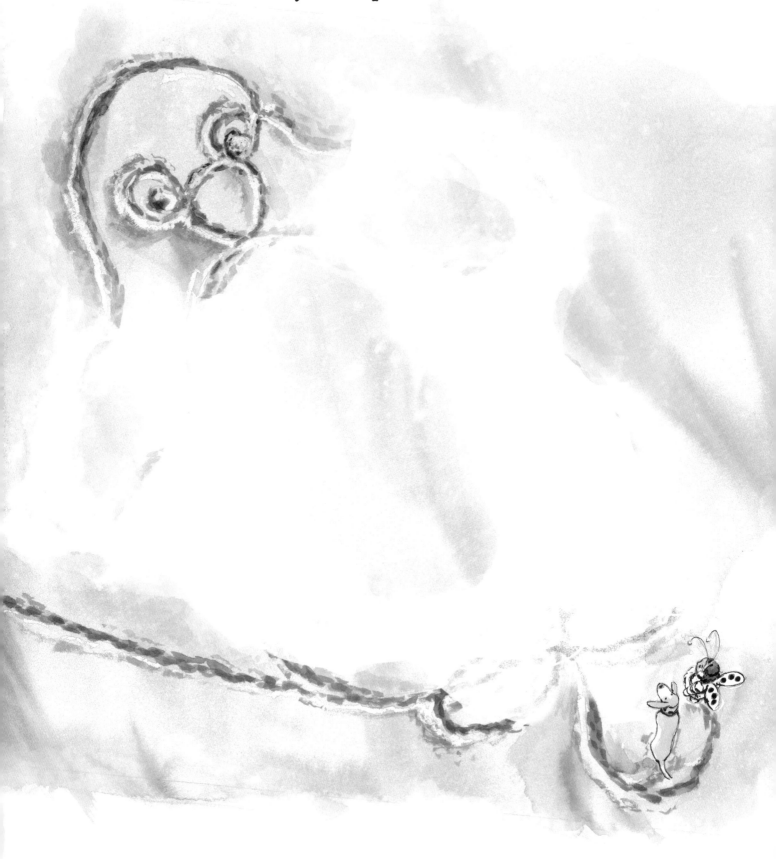

The playground is full of creatures for Ladybug Girl and Bumblebee Boy to watch. Draw the bird they've found sneaking up on Bingo.

Ladybug Girl and Bingo are on the lookout for a family of fairies coming their way. Can you draw the fairies?

Draw all the wildflowers Ladybug Girl has found!
Now she can pick a bunch for Mama!

Wow, look at the night sky!
Can you draw the moon, stars, and planets?

It's been a long day, and it's time to rest!
Draw what Ladybug Girl and Bingo are dreaming about.